TEENAGE MUTANT NINJA TURTLES

THE CASEY CHRONICLES

Published in the United States by Random House Children's Books, a
division of Random House LLC, 1745 Broadway, New York, NY 10019,
and in Canada by Random House of Canada Limited, Toronto, Penguin
Random House Companies. Random House and the colophon are
registered trademarks of Random House LLC. Nickelodeon, Teenage
Mutant Ninja Turtles, and all related titles, logos, and characters are
trademarks of Viacom International Inc. and Viacom Overseas Holdings
C.V. Based on characters created by Peter Laird and Kevin Eastman.

randomhousekids.com

ISBN 978-0-553-50865-9

Printed in the United States of America
10 9 8 7 6 5 4 3 2

THE CASEY CHRONICLES

Adapted by Matthew J. Gilbert

Based on the teleplays
"Target: April O'Neil" by Nicole Dubuc and
"The Good, the Bad, and Casey Jones"
by Johnny Hartmann

RANDOM HOUSE 🏠 NEW YORK

CHAPTER 1

Man, how do I start this thing? I've never had a journal before. I guess I could kick it off with DEAR DIARY.

Nah. Too girly.

What about <u>Awesomeness Journal</u>? I could open with "Welcome to Awesomeness Journal! I'm your host—"

Never mind. That sounds like a TV show. And as crazy as the words on these pages are gonna be, I guarantee you this isn't a TV show. This is as real as it gets.

Oh, I know! How about <u>True Life Memoirs of a Teenage Bounty Hunter</u>?

That sounds totally killer. I could write a bunch of case numbers at the top and mark them solved or unsolved. Maybe include a picture or two of me and my prisoner paper-clipped to the top? You'll look at it all impressed and be like, "Wow, he caught THAT SUPER-DANGEROUS BAD GUY ALL ON HIS OWN? Clearly he did! Look at the photographic proof!"

Crud. Wait a sec.

I forgot; I don't own a camera.

You know what? I'll just start this up by introducing myself. The name's Casey.

Casey Jones.

And these are <u>The Casey Chronicles.</u>

On the off chance you've never heard of me, let me enlighten you. I'm the best hockey player Roosevelt High has ever seen. Ever since I was old enough to play sports, all I wanted to do was

put on a mask and a jersey and hit somebody. I've got some sick skate moves and a major gift for the stick. Nothing can take me out of a game.

Except trigonometry.

Oh, who's that, you ask? Is that an exchange student named Vladimir Trigonometry?

No. I'm talking about the actual subject trigonometry. It's like a math-splosion of numbers and letters. It's a bunch of formulas and junk that make my head hurt worse than a puck straight to the jaw.

I'm flunking hard-core. And Mr. Frowny-Face School Principal said he'd throw me off the hockey team if I don't pass this semester.

So I needed a tutor. And that's how I started hanging out with Red. You probably know her as April O'Neil.

CHAPTER 2

Shredder might have left the country on urgent business, but his presence still ruled over his minions back home.

No one felt this more than his daughter, Karai. Although her father was thousands of miles away, she found herself staring at him, thanks to a video feed broadcast by the M.O.U.S.E.R.S., small robots with projectors in their skulls. The droids' transmission cast Shredder's face in a pixelated glow, making him appear more monstrous than usual. And magnified to the size of a movie theater screen, his disappointment was all the more obvious.

Karai hung her head in shame.

"So, Daughter," Shredder's voice boomed. "Not only do you disobey my orders in my absence, but your petty scheme failed miserably."

Karai knew she was in deep trouble. Over the past few weeks, she had tried to make her father proud by doing her best to capture the Teenage Mutant Ninja Turtles. She knew it wasn't her responsibility, but she wanted to be the one to exact vengeance upon them.

She just didn't have the right tools for the job.

"It was those stupid Footbots!" she protested, staring daggers at the inadequate ninja robots that surrounded her. "They couldn't keep up with the Turtles. But one good thing: the Kraang have been upgrading them! So—"

"Hear me, Karai," Shredder growled. "You will have no more dealings with the Kraang until I return."

"Understood, Father."

"Wait for my command and do not defy me again. The consequences would be . . . unfortunate."

Karai clenched her fists in anger. She couldn't

be seen as a failure—not by the Foot, and especially not by her father. It was time for drastic measures.

And waiting for permission was not an option.

Karai led two Footbots down a long tunnel, mulling over her plans. She was intent on making things right, and for that, she needed the extra-dimensional beings called the Kraang. They were scientists, soldiers, and notorious criminals known throughout the universe. And ever since Shredder had saved them from the wreckage of their space station, they were considered allies.

They still give me the creeps, Karai thought.

Even though Shredder had struck an unlikely alliance with these slimy invaders, she felt uneasy around them: they were cooperating for the moment, but they were also aliens with their own agenda.

Karai and her bots finally arrived at the lab. Kraang-droids, the metallic exoskeletons that housed the brainlike Kraang, patrolled the area.

Other Kraang floated in mobile pods, free to swing their tentacles wherever they pleased. A dome in the middle of the room was hardwired into various computers.

With the flip of a switch, steps materialized out of thin air. Karai climbed them to an observation deck as the dome opened. Smoke billowed out, and a giant robot rose from the floor. Its form was familiar to her: a suit of armor adorned with jagged spikes. It wasn't even powered up, but it sent a shiver along Karai's spine. It was the ultimate in cybernetic warfare: a Dark Ninja Robot.

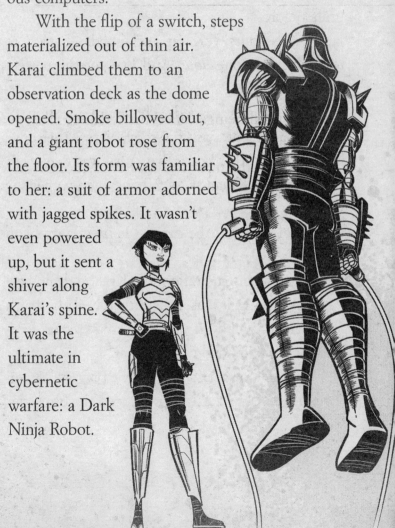

"Not bad," Karai said. "How soon until it's online?"

One Kraang-droid stepped forward to answer her. "By Kraang's calculations, nine Earth-hour units before—"

"Nine hours?" Karai exclaimed. "I want to test it on someone *now*. And I've got the perfect target . . . April O'Neil."

The Kraang gasped. The mere mention of April's name sent a psychic shock across their hive mind. Karai didn't know that April was the key to funneling the Kraang's telekinetic energy, that she was their secret weapon.

Karai glared at the droid. "Is there a problem with that?"

Sensing her frustration, the Kraang-droid hesitated, knowing it was unsafe to reveal the truth about April. Finally, it said, "Kraang sees no foreseeable problem, one called Karai."

"Good. Now let's speed up the process," Karai demanded. "You don't want to keep the Shredder waiting."

In a city of over eight million people, April O'Neil felt totally alone.

She didn't really speak to any of her classmates at school. She avoided making small talk with her teachers. And since her father's unfortunate mutation, she had done her best to ignore her former best friends, the Teenage Mutant Ninja Turtles.

April was mad at the world, so being on her own was exactly what she wanted. She walked down the street, keeping to the shadows, enjoying the silence. She didn't realize that high above her head, someone was leaping from rooftop to rooftop, tracking her every move.

April entered a dark alley and heard a loud

thump behind her. She tried to shrug it off, but some insistent rustling told her she had company. She turned to look and caught a glimpse of green out of the corner of her eye.

"I know you're following me!" April shouted, whipping out her trusty *tessen*. "Come out so I can see you!"

But her mystery stalker didn't answer. April scanned the area, choosing her moment carefully. She took a breath and, just as Master Splinter had taught her, expertly launched the fan.

The war fan flew and—*wham!*—clocked her target square on the head, forcing him into the light.

It was Donatello.

April's face clouded over with anger. "Donnie?"

Donnie froze. He hadn't spoken to April since the incident: a canister of mutagen had doused Kirby O'Neil in green goo, turning him into a grotesque creature of the night. That accident had ended Donnie and April's friendship. Donnie went for his emergency plan: act as casual as possible.

"Hey, it's funny how we both happen to be

passing through this shady alley at the same time," he said, striking a not-very-relaxed pose. "So . . . how've you been?"

"Oh, you know, the usual," April replied. "Homework, chess club, dealing with a father who turned into a homicidal mutant bat!"

"April, it wasn't our fault," Donnie insisted. "I'm sorry that—"

"Not as sorry as I am! I want to be left alone, Donnie! No more talking mutants in my life. I never want to see you again!"

Donnie winced. He could tell she meant it, and that hurt.

He watched her turn and walk away. Afraid this might be the last time he ever saw her, he tried to reason with her.

"April!" he cried. "Some things are just beyond our control."

But it was no use. April just kept walking.

CHAPTER 4

Heartbroken, Donnie wandered back to the Turtles' lair, hoping to have some quiet time in the lab. Unfortunately, his brothers had other plans for the evening. Leonardo, Raphael, and Michelangelo were surrounding the television, settling in for a marathon of *Super Robo Mecha Force Five,* an anime show Donnie absolutely hated.

"Great," Donnie mumbled to himself. "And I thought my night couldn't get any worse."

Too tired to complain, Donnie sat quietly and watched: Princess, one of the best space pilots, was angry with the rest of her team for forgetting her birthday. It hurt her feelings so much that she quit the Force.

As much as he hated to relate to this show, Donnie winced. He knew exactly how it felt to see a best friend and trusted teammate slip away. He feared that things with April would never be the same.

Mikey looked up from the screen at Donnie. "Whoa, dude, this show, like, totally *paradoxes* your life! Kinda owie in the *corazón*." He paused, then added, "By the way, *corazón* means 'heart.'"

"You mean *parallels,* not *paradoxes,*" Donnie corrected him. "And it has nothing to do with me. It's just a cartoon."

Leo tried to defuse the situation. "Princess has quit the team like twenty-seven times!" he explained, remembering the last few episodes they'd watched. "She *always* comes back."

"Yeah, but let's face reality," Raph said, realizing who they were really talking about. "April's gone for good. We'll probably never see her again."

Donnie shuddered at the thought. He couldn't bear the idea of losing April forever.

"I'll be in my lab," he sighed.

The moment he walked through the doors to

the lab, he noticed a strange purple light blinking across the room.

"The Kraang communicator!" Donnie inspected the machine their outer-space adversaries used to transmit messages. The Turtles had recovered one from the sewers shortly before the Kraang tried to invade Earth. After weeks of radio silence, the alien device was pulsating with life once again.

"Guys!" Donnie yelled. "We have a problem!"

CHAPTER 5

The Turtles patrolled the streets in their vehicle, the *Shellraiser*, looking for signs of the Kraang. Donnie stared at a stack of papers in his lap, trying to stay focused. He needed to stop thinking about April long enough to wrap his head around these Kraang translations he'd decoded. After all, it wasn't like April was thinking about him at that exact moment.

Wait, is she? No. Stop it! Donnie scolded himself. *Get your head out of your shell!* He zeroed in on the numbers on the page before him.

"From what I could translate from the orb," he explained, "it seems the Kraang are building some kind of advanced heavy weaponry."

Leo looked up from the road. "Any guess what it could be?"

In the back of the van, Mikey's hand shot up like he was trying to catch the teacher's eye in a classroom. "Oooh!" he exclaimed, convinced he had the answer. "Lasers disguised as . . . *burritos!* Yes! It all makes sense now."

Mikey's "solution" was met with silence and eye-rolls.

Raph knew how to handle this. He unbuckled his seat belt and approached Mikey. "It *does* make sense," he said, "if you have an avocado for a brain!"

"All right, guys," Leo said from the front seat. "Let's stay focused."

Everyone took a breath and returned to his battle station. It was time to get serious. The Kraang were out there, and that was bigger than any brotherly bickering or moping that was happening.

"We find the weapon and destroy it," Leo told his brothers. After a brief pause, he added, "And then we get Mexican pizza." All this talk of burritos and avocados had made him really hungry.

They all smiled. Finally, something they could agree on!

Our first study session was a walk in the park.

Literally.

Apparently, Red loves to study at the park. She said she's been doing it for a few years. The fresh air helps her think clearly or something.

It didn't help me any. Because all I could think was HOLY COW, THIS STUDY SESSION FEELS LIKE A DATE. But, no worries. Just like on the ice, I was totally ready.

Deodorant? Check.

Best punk rock T-shirt? Double check.

Hanging out with the cutest girl

at Roosevelt High on the swing set?
Triple check.

That's CASEY JONES FOR THE HAT
TRICK!

I feel like we learned about each
other. Like, I learned that Red is a
Science Olympian. And I told her
that I want to grow up to be a
professional hockey star or
international bounty hunter.

Yeah, okay, I'll admit she did try
to make me answer a few trig
questions, but I told her school
wasn't really my thing. So we just
hung out. And then, as if our
date couldn't get any better . . .

I SAVED HER FROM THE
COOLEST-LOOKING MONSTER I'VE
EVER SEEN!

This thing had to be at least
twenty feet tall. Eyes and
internal organs all mixed

up and floating around in
a box like a big spaghetti mess.
It was totally jacked
up, though. Diesel

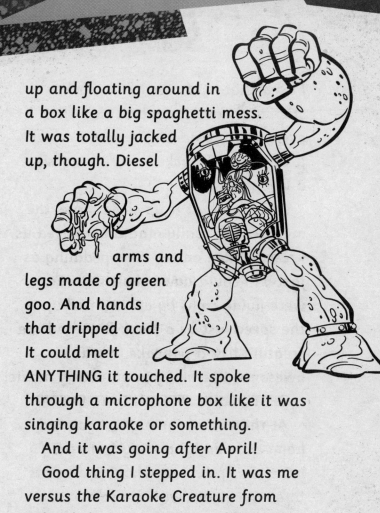

arms and
legs made of green
goo. And hands
that dripped acid!
It could melt
ANYTHING it touched. It spoke
through a microphone box like it was
singing karaoke or something.

And it was going after April!

Good thing I stepped in. It was me
versus the Karaoke Creature from
Behind the Dumpster. I grabbed a lead
pipe and went all GOONGALA on it!
(Well, maybe Red helped a little bit.)

BUT I TOOK IT DOWN LIKE A BOSS.

I used that lead pipe like a hockey
stick and gave it my best slap shot. I
even shot the garbage around me at
it like hockey pucks—everything was
a weapon!

After we beat it up some more, the
monster got really mad and chased us.
I rescued Red on my bike, pedaling as
fast as I could down the street. Cars
were flying right by us! I turned up
the speed just as a truck flattened the
creature like a pancake. It was so
awesome, like being in an action movie!
BEST STUDY SESSION/DATE EVER!!!

At the end of the night, I got Red
home safe and far away from the
monster. And guess what? She wants
to go out again with me tomorrow
night! WOOHOO!!

Maybe we'll even get some studying
done.

It was late at night, and Casey Jones had the
rink all to himself. He skated speed drills.
He practiced his wrist shot. He even made
his own audience sound effects
whenever he scored a goal.

Life was good on the ice.

Just as he was prepping
another puck for launch,
he noticed a figure
moving in the stands.
Someone else had
entered the
rink, and
judging by her petite frame and

messenger bag, she wasn't another player.

It was April.

"Red?" Casey skated over to her. "Did I miss a study session again?"

"No . . ." She hesitated, as if trying to find the right words. "I'm just here to . . . hang out."

"With the infamous Casey Jones?" he asked with a smirk as he skated backward.

"Unless you only like me for my trigonometry skills," April joked.

They both laughed. Neither of them had said it yet, but they were becoming more than just study partners. They felt like . . . friends.

The two exchanged an awkward stare. Casey could tell April had something on her mind.

"So what's your deal?" Casey finally asked. "I never see you hanging out with anybody. Anti-social much?"

Things got awkward again.

"Not really," April murmured.

She wanted to tell him everything—about the Turtles, her mutant-bat dad, the alien encounters—

but she didn't want to scare off the first human she'd befriended in years. Still, it would be nice to talk to *someone*.

"I . . . I had four really close friends," she confessed, careful to keep her answer vague but honest. "I don't talk to them anymore."

Casey nodded. He understood what that was like. "It happens. Me and my best friend, Nick, were up against Troma Town in last year's playoffs, right?" He fired a puck that clanged off the cross-bar. "He came up behind me just as I was about to sink the winning goal and *wham!* My stick caught him in the face; it smacked his helmet straight off! Swollen face, split lip . . . My best friend since second grade . . . Never spoke to me again."

Casey looked down at his skates. It was a bad memory he didn't like reliving. April tried to comfort him.

"It's not like you meant it," she said.

"Right," Casey responded, staring off into the distance. "Some stuff is just . . . beyond our control."

April's eyes widened; Donnie's words from

earlier echoed in her head. Seeing how sad Casey was helped her understand how the Turtles must have felt. Her face clouded over with guilt. *Did I push the Turtles away for the wrong reasons?*

Casey stepped off the ice and got close. "Give me a sec to grab my gear. We can get something to eat. Pizza?"

Pizza. Yet another thing that reminded her of the Turtles. April couldn't lie to herself anymore: she missed her Teenage Mutant Ninja Turtle friends.

As Casey disappeared into the locker room, she grabbed her old T-Phone from her bag and pulled up Donnie's picture in the contacts list. There he was—all smiles underneath that purple mask. It reminded her of happier times. She touched his face affectionately and sighed.

KABLAM!

An explosion jostled April back to reality. The ground rumbled, and chunks of plaster flew through the air. As the dust cleared, she saw the outlines of two shadowy intruders. She recognized their black ninja masks and red bandanas.

"Foot Soldiers!" she exclaimed.

They charged at her, swinging blades and throwing punches. April did her best to dodge them, lurching left and right in the stands, narrowly avoiding their strikes. They seemed faster and stronger than she remembered.

Suddenly, blades and spikes popped out of their backs. Their eyes lit up.

Impossible, April thought. "Didn't you guys used to be human?" she screamed at them.

April needed a plan. These weren't the clumsy Foot Soldiers she was used to. She rolled backward and, deciding to take her chances, lured them onto the ice. But the two Foot Soldiers never lost their balance! They skated toward her with ease. April's plan had backfired, but just as they were about to surround her, all the overhead lights came to life.

"Yo!" a voice called from across the ice. The Foot Soldiers turned to see a red jersey coming up fast.

It was Casey!

"If there's one thing I have, it's crackerjack timing," he called out.

"Casey, run!" April screamed.

"What? So you get all the fun?" Casey teed up two pucks and unleashed them directly at the ninjas' faces. The soldiers tumbled to the ice.

"I got 'em," he told April. "You go!"

But April wasn't going anywhere. She unsheathed her *tessen* and took a fighting stance.

"No, *I* got 'em! *You* go!" she replied.

The moment the attackers got back up, Casey sliced across the ice and threw his own body like a human projectile. One Foot Soldier was thrown into the glass.

"Cross-checking!" Casey shouted, calling the penalty like a sports announcer. "Two minutes!"

Casey went after the other one, wielding his hockey stick like a club. He pulled back and hit him with all the rage in his body. The Foot Soldier fell headfirst onto the ice, sparks sputtering out of its head. "High sticking!" Casey shouted. Then, with a smile, he added, "Hey, it ain't a penalty if they deserve it, right?"

Before he could say anything else, the first Foot Soldier took Casey by surprise and knocked him onto the ice. As it raised a scythelike weapon over Casey's head, April saw her opportunity. She reached over and grabbed the other Foot Soldier's discarded blades. With a mighty throw, she landed a one-in-a-million shot, striking the soldier down for good. Purple sparks shot out of its body.

These Foot Soldiers are definitely not human, she realized.

"You got some serious rink rage, Red," Casey said.

"You should see me play table tennis," April replied.

"So . . . you owe these guys money or something?"

"Or *something*," she said, suddenly hearing more footsteps all around them. April looked up.

More Footbots! It was an ambush! The strange robotic ninjas hit the ice and began fanning out in an attack pattern.

"Casey, just go," April pleaded. "I didn't mean to get you into this."

"Are you kidding me?" Casey yelled. "Do you know what this is? This is Casey Jones versus Evil Robo-Ninjas! It's the coolest freaking thing in the universe!"

With his hockey stick held high, Casey skated into battle, yelling his signature war cry: *"GOON-GALA!"*

Before April could protest, Casey had lured the Footbots far away from her. He was easily outnumbered. Their buzzing saw blades overpowered him, slicing his stick in two. April knew she had to do something. The Foot were clearly after her and her alone. She didn't want to be the reason Casey got hurt.

I won't lose another friend, she thought.

"Hey, Footbots! You want me? Come and get me!" April cried, doing her best to distract them.

Casey tried to stop her. "April!"

But it was too late. She was already off the ice, sprinting for her life, leading most of the Footbots out of the rink in the process.

Casey looked back at his opponents, sizing up the competition: just three Footbots left on the ice. He liked his odds now. He picked up a shiny new hockey stick.

"Now the fight's fair," Casey said.

He lined up more hockey pucks. He swung hard and screamed, "Eat this!"

CHAPTER 7

April bolted out of the hockey rink, making her way toward an adjacent alley. She glanced over her shoulder: the Footbots were in hot pursuit.

One of them flung ninja blades at April. She stopped short and ducked. The steel knives flew inches above her head and dug into a brick wall.

April saw an opportunity. She climbed the blades like a miniature stairway up the wall of an apartment building! About ten feet up, she grabbed onto a fire escape ladder and kept climbing until she reached the safety of the rooftop.

It was an impressive ninja feat. And one that had not gone unnoticed.

Across the street, a mysterious watcher stood

atop a water tower, following April's escape through a pair of binoculars.

It was Karai.

The Shredder's ruthless daughter was seeing her evil plan come together. She had successfully flushed April out into the open after weeks of hiding underground. Now it was time for Phase Two.

"She's traveling north on the rooftops," Karai informed her Footbots. "Move!"

The army of robots wordlessly followed her orders, tracking their human target. It was time to eliminate April O'Neil!

CHAPTER 8

While April was running away from the Foot-bots, the Turtles were running out of options. They were hiding in the shadows, staking out what they believed to be a secret Kraang lab.

"That's our entry point," Leo said. "We just need a distraction."

The other Turtles racked their brains for ideas. They knew they had to sneak in fast and undetected, but a number of strange men in suits were guarding the door. The Turtles recognized them as Normans—Kraang-droids disguised as human businessmen.

Mikey studied the billboard lights above them. It was like a literal lightbulb going on in his brain. "Dude, I got the best plan!" he gushed.

Leo, Donnie, and Raph all turned at once to look at him with surprise.

"Why do I feel slightly nauseated?" Raph scoffed.

"Check it out," Mikey said, adjusting the billboard light. He put his hands in front of the bulb and started making shadow puppets. "I've been practicing."

And with that, a gigantic shadow danced across the Kraang's hideout. The Normans saw a twenty-foot-tall rabbit hopping over their heads!

"Kraang, creatures known as rabbits have infiltrated Kraang's lab," one Norman observed.

And before the others could respond, the shadowy creature morphed into a wild elephant!

"No, Kraang," another Norman said, identifying the new animal. "Clearly a small but obese pachyderm has breached Kraang security."

The elephant disappeared, and the slinky silhouette of a woman appeared. The monumental figure turned and spun gracefully before them.

"Kraang are both wrong!" a different Norman announced, scanning his mental database for answers. "It is a dancer wearing what is known as a flamenco dress."

With all the Normans distracted, Leo, Donnie, and Raph saw their opportunity. They drew their weapons and leaped down from the fire escape, taking out droids before the chrome domes even knew what hit them!

Leo was impressed. It wasn't often that Mikey's insane plans worked, but he had to hand it to his little brother this time. "You've got some mad shadow-puppetry skills."

"Like a Turtle do!" Mikey bragged with a smile.

Raph helped Donnie up to an open window. Once he gave the all clear, the other Turtles somersaulted their way up to join him.

They were in.

The Turtles walked cautiously down a long, dark corridor. Though the building they entered

looked like an abandoned warehouse from the outside, the inside made them feel like they had been transported to another world. Purple-pink lights buzzed all around them. Strange alien symbols decorated their surroundings. Up ahead, they saw the sterile white light of a lab.

This was definitely a Kraang hideout.

Beyond the usual Kraang-droids and free-floating Kraang brains that went about their business, Donnie saw something in the center of the room that he'd never seen before: a robotic creation made in Shredder's image. It had the same mask and spikes, but he figured it would have even more strength.

"I'm guessing we just found the secret weapon," Donnie whispered.

"All right, Donnie, we need you to shut that thing down," Leo said.

"No problem!"

Suddenly, a loud buzzing noise started. Had they been spotted? The Turtles ducked, scanning the area for the source of the sound.

Mikey pointed: it was Donnie's shell!

"Dude, you're vibrating," Mikey said.

Donnie scrambled for his T-Phone, remembering he'd put it on vibrate mode earlier. *This is embarrassing,* he thought—until he saw who was calling!

"It's April!" he exclaimed.

He took a breath and tried to play it cool as he answered: "Hi, this is—"

He was so nervous he couldn't even say his own name!

"This is Dona-Deener-Don-Donna-Dino—"

"Donnie!" he heard her scream. "Remember how you said sometimes things are out of our control? Well, you were right! Things are really out of control right now!"

April screamed so loud over the T-Phone, they all heard it.

Donnie turned to his brothers. "She needs me, guys!" And then he spoke into the phone: "Hold on, April! I'll be right there!"

"Donnie," Leo protested, "*we* need your help!"

But it was too late. Donnie abandoned the other Turtles to save April.

Raph could feel himself getting angrier than usual. "He ditched *us*?"

And then, as if on cue, an alarm sounded and a computer voice boomed over the speakers: "Alerting of one known as Intruder!"

The Turtles saw every creature in the room come to a standstill. Their cover wasn't just blown—it was about to be blown *away*! Every Kraang-droid sprang into action. They opened fire with a barrage of laser blasts.

"Turtles, attack!" Leo commanded.

Leo, Raph, and Mikey unsheathed their weapons. They might have been short one Turtle, but they weren't going down without a fight.

CHAPTER 9

Casey Jones had been on the ice for many years, but he'd never seen action like this. He teed up a few more pucks and skated toward the three Footbots still standing in his way. He was running on pure adrenaline. He felt like more than a hockey player.

He felt like a hero.

"Wrist shot!" Casey called out, striking down two Footbots with a lightning-fast trick play. He readied the next puck and swung with fury. "Slap shot!"

The disc flew like a missile, knocking the final Footbot down on the ice.

Casey laughed, taunting his attackers: "You might wanna get that looked at!"

The Footbots collected themselves. Their learning technology enabled them to study Casey's movements and mimic them instantly—which meant they were now skating like pros! The bots glided around the net, throwing blades that hummed at Casey with scary precision.

Casey dodged the flying knives. He was preparing a perfect high-speed body check.

THWACK! The hit was so hard a bot's head came loose! Casey caught it with his stick and fired into the net!

"One–zip!" Casey celebrated. "Home ice leads! Who's next?"

The remaining Footbots drew backup weapons, but it didn't faze Casey at this point. These robo-ninjas were on his turf, and on this ice, he had a reputation for being undefeated.

"Come get some," Casey told them.

April couldn't run anymore. Her legs felt like jelly, and she was out of breath. But she couldn't stop. One relentless Footbot chased her off the main street to the park.

She climbed over the merry-go-round, narrowly escaping the bot's grasp. She ran toward the shadows, searching for a place to hide until the Turtles arrived.

Then she heard something cut through the eerie quiet—a familiar buzzing sound like a spinning saw.

She turned, hearing another set of blades.

And another.

It was a trap! A squad of Footbots surrounded her, each ready to slice-and-dice her with his saw blade. April knew there was no escape. All she could see was a wall of ninjas encircling her in the dark.

This was no random attack, she realized. Someone had programmed these robots to lure her here. But who? And for what purpose?

April wanted answers. In spite of being outnumbered, she stood her ground, drawing her *tessen.*

"Fine," she said defiantly. "You want a fight?"

But out of nowhere, a Footbot snuck up on her and pinned her arms behind her back. Her war fan fell limply to the ground. April's fight was over. But the Foot's was just getting started.

The bots moved in unison, like a pack of wolves, closing in on her from all sides. More weapons began to appear: an arsenal of scythes, *katanas,* and spikes. The bots' eyes burned red.

April struggled to break free, but the Footbot held her with an iron grip. April feared her bones might break under the pressure. She winced, bracing for the worst. . . .

But a familiar weapon pierced the Footbot right in front of her. The bot collapsed into a heap of scrap metal.

"Donnie!" April exclaimed. He was holding the *bo* staff that had just saved her life. The same one that was about to finish off the rest of the Footbots.

In a blur of green, Donnie somersaulted through the air, taking out Footbot after Footbot. He cracked their CPUs with his staff, then stomped their circuits into oblivion. Donnie deployed his secret *bo* staff blade and destroyed the bot holding April with a sharp strike.

"Took you long enough," April joked, with a sigh of relief.

"I'm sorry! I had to figure out your coordinates on the T-Phone—"

Before Donnie could finish his thought, two ninja stars flew at them.

Karai!

Shredder's daughter was flanked by more Footbots. "Well, I was hoping for *all* the Turtles to see this . . . but I guess one's good enough."

Donnie readied his *bo* staff once more. He'd just gotten April back in his life, and he wasn't about to lose her again!

CHAPTER 10

At that exact moment, Leo, Raph, and Mikey were facing down a hailstorm of blaster fire. White-hot lasers whizzed by their shells as they fanned out.

Leo was the first to strike. The incoming blasts were so rapid he had no choice but to keep his distance and launch ninja stars. He could hear the metal projectiles connect with a screech. He vaulted forward and unsheathed his trusty *katanas,* slicing a droid at the knees.

Raph bolted next. He surprised two Kraang-droids with a stiff-arm *sai* attack.

The Turtles were feeling pretty good . . . until a dozen more Kraang-droids arrived. The fresh droids shot up the room, leaving a trail of destruction in their wake.

Mikey took a deep breath and sprang into action. He released the secret chain from his *nunchucks* and caught the barrel of a Kraang-droid's blaster in one swift move. The droid squeezed the trigger, releasing a steady bombardment of laser-fire. Mikey quickly pulled back on the chain and spun the droid. The whirling dervish took out every other droid in the room. Their systems were fried before their exoskeletons hit the floor.

Leo dispatched the final shooter with a crane kick. Victory was theirs!

All that was left were a few defenseless Kraang brains in their tiny floating pods. These aliens hovered around their dormant cybernetic secret weapon, the Dark Ninja Robot. They tapped some commands into their computers.

The Dark Ninja Robot looked exactly like Shredder. It stood nearly eight feet tall, with barbaric proportions and a steely mask.

Mikey couldn't believe how cool it was. "Whoa, that thing is awesome!" he exclaimed. And then he added, "In an evil kind of way."

The sound of popping cables and depressurized air startled them all back to reality. A cluster of wires detached from the Dark Ninja Robot, allowing its platform to shift so its boots could touch the ground.

It was powering up!

"Ummm, guys," Leo said nervously. "The giant robo-ninja just finished charging!"

Its eyes suddenly glowed red.

"You don't look so tough!" Mikey yelled as he ran toward it, spinning his *nunchucks*. He went airborne for a dive attack, when—

The Dark Ninja Robot's head snapped up to attention, tracking Mikey's trajectory. A shape made of brilliant light materialized in its hand. It was a thin, curved beam crackling with white-hot energy.

It was a plasma whip!

The robot cracked it masterfully, slashing Mikey to the floor with a thud.

Raph gasped. "Mikey!"

The Dark Ninja Robot's head swiveled toward

Raph. Its red eyes emitted a heat ray! Raph cart-wheeled out of its scorching path.

Leo joined Raph for a two-on-one battle. Both Turtles pulled their weapons, ready to attack. But the robot had something else up its sleeve—*literally!* With a flick of its wrist, it suddenly released a plasma sword!

The Dark Ninja Robot parried every one of Leo's sword strikes, knocking him down again and again. This gave Raph enough time to jump up and land on the robot's back, digging his *sais* into its spiked shoulder mounts.

But the robot was unharmed. It tossed Raph into the air, then kicked him like a rag doll. As Raph lay wounded, he heard Leo reenter the fight. He charged bravely with his *katanas.* But the Dark Ninja Robot caught him with its plasma whip, slapping him down with an electric jolt.

Leo was shell-shocked and unable to move. The plasma whip tightened around him, searing his arms and sending electric shocks through his body.

"Let me go!" he groaned.

The Dark Ninja Robot lumbered toward him, its eyes burning red with heat. Nothing was going to stop it from vaporizing the Turtles!

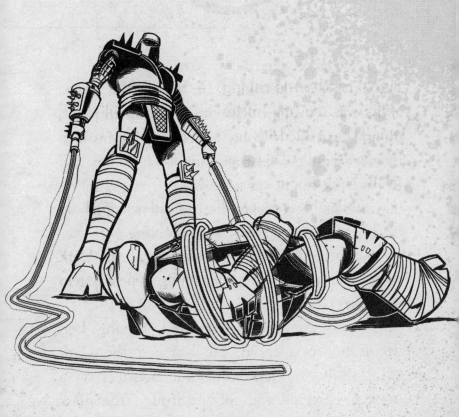

CHAPTER 11

Leo's heart was racing. He felt like the plasma whip was roasting his insides and scrambling his mind. He gritted his teeth, trying to stay strong, trying to think of a way out. But it was no use. The Dark Ninja Robot came closer.

Suddenly, it stopped. Its head snapped up awkwardly, almost like it was rebooting.

"Subroutine program taking over," the Dark Ninja Robot said aloud, confirming its new system priorities. "April O'Neil located."

The plasma whip retracted, freeing Leo from its stranglehold. He watched the Dark Ninja Robot's boots ignite like boosters on a rocket, carrying the robot through the glass ceiling with the speed of a missile.

"It's going after April!" Raph said. "C'mon!"

Raph helped Leo up and headed for the exit.
Mikey was about to follow when he noticed a
Kraang blaster on the floor. He excitedly picked it
up. "Too awesome!" he said, squeezing off a few
blasts by accident. The weapon was so powerful
he could barely control it. Energy bolts flew everywhere, a few nearly zapping Raph and Leo!

They turned angrily, staring daggers at Mikey
from the exit.

Mikey gulped. He gently set the blaster down
on the floor and decided to stick with his *nunchucks*.

Unaware that his brothers were on their way to
back him up, Donnie was bracing himself to face
an army of Footbots alone. If that was what he had
to do to protect April from Karai, then so be it.

"Stay away from April!" he warned Karai.

Karai's lips curled into a smile. "Footbots,
keep the Turtle busy!"

All around him, Footbots swarmed in an attack formation, making it hard for Donnie to cover April. He had no choice but to break away and take them on. He swung his *bo* staff, clocking one bot upside his dome and scissor-kicking another. As he traded punches with two more bots, Karai cat-walked across their shoulders, making a beeline for April.

"This is between us girls," Karai said, landing gracefully before April in a fighting stance. She twirled a scythe and readied its blade.

Anger filled April. She had bested Karai once, knocking her down a subway stairwell. She could do it again.

April pulled out her *tessen*. The two *kunoichi* began to brawl—their fight picked up right where it had left off. After swapping a few jabs and kicks, Karai booted April to the cement with a bicycle kick.

April yelped in pain, rolling away to safety just as Karai's scythe came down, cracking the ground. April tossed her fan.

It whiffed wildly into the air, missing Karai by a mile.

A wicked smile played over Karai's face. "Your skills are weak, April: I've had years of training—"

THWACK!

The fan darted back like a boomerang, nailing Karai in the jaw. She was stunned into silence as she watched April catch the fan like a pro.

"You talk too much," April told her with a smirk. But there was no time to gloat. Karai was enraged. She charged April with her scythe and knocked her down, the scythe blade swatting away the fan.

April was defenseless. She raised her hand in front of her face, anticipating a vicious attack.

WHAM! Donnie's staff came down just in time to shield April from Karai's blade.

"You're not gonna touch her!" Donnie yelled. He whacked the scythe out of her hands and unleashed an expert-level *kata* that sent her stumbling backward.

Now it was Karai who was defenseless.

Donnie spun his *bo* staff, moving in for a finishing blow, when he noticed something odd swooping through the sky—it looked like something out of a comic book: an armored man with rocket boosters on the bottoms of his shoes.

But as the flying figure came closer, Donnie realized it wasn't human at all. He took in its over-sized proportions and glowing red eyes. Then he recognized it as the Kraang's secret weapon: the Dark Ninja Robot.

And it was coming in for a landing.

Donnie's jaw dropped. He had never seen weaponry so advanced.

April shivered at the sight of the robo-monstrosity. "Donnie, I'm thinking . . . *retreat!*"

As April and Donnie gazed at the robot's fearsome face, Karai collected herself and walked with a newfound confidence. Her protector—her *creation*—had been completed and was here to do her evil bidding.

"Like my new toy?" Karai asked, her eyes meeting April's. She couldn't have been happier that the time had come to field-test her little battle machine. She turned back to the Dark Ninja Robot and commanded: "Robot, eliminate the girl!"

Knowing he had to protect April, Donnie sized up the Dark Ninja Robot, trying to figure out the best plan of attack. He knew it could fly, but could it fight?

Donnie spun his *bo* staff and charged forward. He swung full-force at the robot's head, but the Dark Ninja Robot was too quick for that. With a simple, effortless move, the robot caught Donnie's staff in midair.

April tried to run, but something started pulling her back. She felt a hot, almost-liquid substance bundling her arms together. She couldn't move. She couldn't breathe. A bright crackle of energy coiled around her like a glowing rope. It was the Dark Ninja Robot's plasma whip!

"Let me go!" April pleaded.

She tried to wriggle free, but it was no use. The Dark Ninja Robot was much too strong.

She waited for the robot to finish her off. Lucky for her, it had a sophisticated ID scanner. It quickly recognized her.

"System override," the Dark Ninja Robot announced. "Do not destroy April O'Neil. Capture for the Kraang!"

And with that, the Dark Ninja Robot activated its thrusters and began to fly away with April in tow!

Karai gasped. This wasn't the plan! Using her spear, she knocked the robot off its flight path, bringing it and April to the ground with a thud.

The Dark Ninja Robot studied Karai. "Threat detected," it announced. "Eliminate threat."

Karai backed up cautiously.

Seeing his opportunity, Donnie ran past the robot to April.

"Are you okay?" he asked, helping her up.

"For once," April began with a relieved smile, "I'm actually glad the Kraang want to kidnap me."

CHAPTER

13

Meanwhile, inside the *Shellraiser,* the other Turtles kicked their rescue efforts into high gear with the help of their best tracking device. They finally had a bead on April's coordinates.

"Left, Leo!" Raph barked from his navigation station. "The signal's getting stronger!"

Leo turned the wheel hard, banking around a corner and into a park. It wasn't long before the *Shellraiser's* headlights flashed on a familiar figure . . . the Dark Ninja Robot! The metal warrior was gaining ground on April and Donnie.

Leo hit the brakes, cut the wheel, and sent the *Shellraiser* spinning into a high-speed three-sixty. At fifty miles per hour, the vehicle was like an unstoppable wrecking ball of pure steel, slamming into the Dark Ninja Robot and sending it flying through the air. It hit a nearby brick wall with a crash, the impact frying some of its core circuits.

"Oh, yeah!" Mikey cheered. "Firing manhole covers!"

Mikey squeezed the trigger and opened fire on the Dark Ninja Robot. A barrage of manhole covers bounced off the robot's face.

Mikey screamed, "Eat it, Chrome Dome!"

The Dark Ninja Robot suddenly stood up, alert. It shook off the damage and activated its heat vision, slicing the incoming manhole covers with ease. The iron disks fell to the cement in cauterized lumps.

Now it was the robot's turn. It lashed out with its plasma whip, catching Mikey off guard in an electrically charged corkscrew. The robot tore Mikey away from his cannon and threw him aside.

Leo and Raph leaped out after him not a moment too soon. The robot made a beeline toward the van and flipped it over. It bounced off a wall with a crash.

Leo watched the *Shellraiser* roll to a halt. It was scrap metal now. "Aw, I just waxed her," he groaned.

It was then that the Dark Ninja Robot resumed its target practice with Karai. The robot went after her with everything in its arsenal: heat vision, plasma whip, and plasma sword.

It was an impressive sight, and Mikey geeked out accordingly.

"Dude, I so want plasma *nunchucks*," Mikey said, salivating over the robot's sizzling weapons. And then, looking up at his tech-savvy brother, Donnie, he added, "Can you hook a Turtle up?"

But Donnie wasn't listening. He was focused on one thing: the exposed wiring on the robot's back! It must have come loose when the *Shellraiser* banged into it. Maybe this cybernetic warrior had a weak spot after all!

"Guys," Donnie announced, "I think I know how we can take that thing down!"

Though it was welcome news at that moment, the other Turtles were still sore about Donnie's bailing on them back at the Kraang lab.

"Oh, are you on this team?" Raph said with a smirk.

"Yeah, way to ditch us, dude!" Leo piled on.

Even Mikey was mad. He blew a raspberry at Donnie.

April piped up over the commotion, coming to his defense. "Go easy on him, guys! If it wasn't for Donnie, I would have—"

Wham! Karai silenced her with a surprise scissor kick to the gut. "I don't need that stupid robot to finish you," Karai yelled. *"Hiyaaa!"*

"April!" Donnie shouted, his heart racing.

Leo stood in his way. "I'll help April," he assured him. "You guys take down—"

"Chrome Dome!" Mikey shouted, completing his brother's sentence. Even in the thick of battle, Mikey didn't want to miss the opportunity to name the bad guy.

As Leo began brawling with Karai, Donnie heard a crash from behind. Then another. And another!

Chrome Dome had finished off the remaining Footbots, throwing their still-sparking parts into a pile of garbage. Now the only things standing between it and April O'Neil were the Turtles!

It was elimination time.

Chrome Dome charged at them, swinging its plasma sword with terrifying precision.

It tracked every one of the Turtles' somersaults and dodges, but it couldn't land a hit. The Turtles' simultaneous ninja moves were too frenzied for the robot. They were nothing but a blur of green.

This allowed Mikey to trap it with his secret *nunchuck* chain! With Raph's help, he wrapped it around Chrome Dome. The robot couldn't move!

Now, it was Donnie's chance to jump in and do a little rewiring.

He leaped onto Chrome Dome's back, tearing away the system panel and ripping out some of its circuits. The robot spun out of control. The Turtles hung on for their lives as the robot's body revolved like a gyrating top, whirling them around and around at supersonic speeds!

The g-forces sent everyone flying to the ground. Mikey pulled himself up, trying to shake off his dizziness. He was seeing double, but one image became clear.

The plasma sword!

It must have been thrown to the ground with everyone else! Mikey grabbed the futuristic weapon as fast as he could. He tightened his grip around the handle, and plunged the white-hot electrical blade into Chrome Dome's back, frying its circuits for good.

The Dark Ninja Robot slowly sputtered, the last of its power draining away with a fading hum.

Mikey smiled, knowing they had pulled the plug on Chrome Dome.

And that wasn't the only battle where the Turtles could claim victory. It was clear that Leo

CASEY JONES

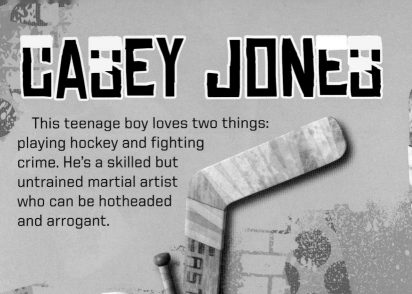

This teenage boy loves two things: playing hockey and fighting crime. He's a skilled but untrained martial artist who can be hotheaded and arrogant.

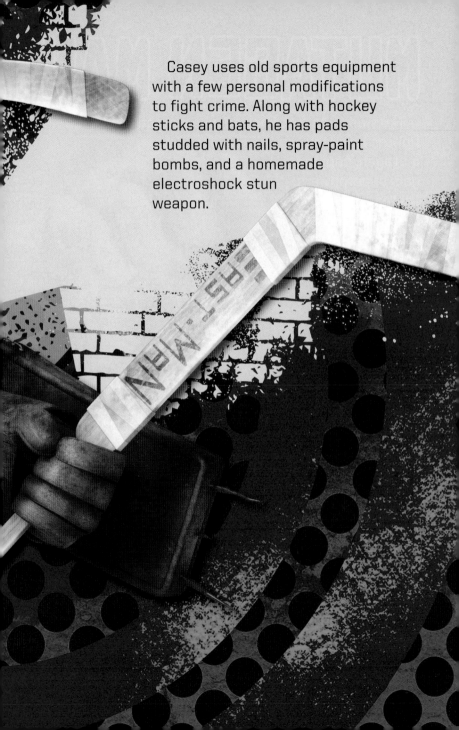

Casey uses old sports equipment with a few personal modifications to fight crime. Along with hockey sticks and bats, he has pads studded with nails, spray-paint bombs, and a homemade electroshock stun weapon.

MUTAGEN MAN

Tim was once a normal kid who wanted to be a crime fighter. He drank mutagen, hoping to gain superpowers. Instead, he became Mutagen Man, a strange blob with an acidic touch.

KIRBY BAT

Mutagen accidentally splashed April O'Neil's father during a rescue attempt by the Turtles. Now he is a giant mutant bat.

FOOTBOTS

The Kraang created these deadly robotic warriors for Shredder. Equipped with sharp weapons for hands, they are programmed with nine hundred different combat styles.

KARAI

Karai is a cunning and strong-willed *kunoichi*, a female ninja. She is very loyal to her teacher and adoptive father, Shredder.

DARK NINJA ROBOT

Chrome Dome is Michelangelo's nickname for this android built by the Kraang. Powerful and deadly, it is equipped with rockets for fast escapes and carries a glowing whip and a giant energy sword.

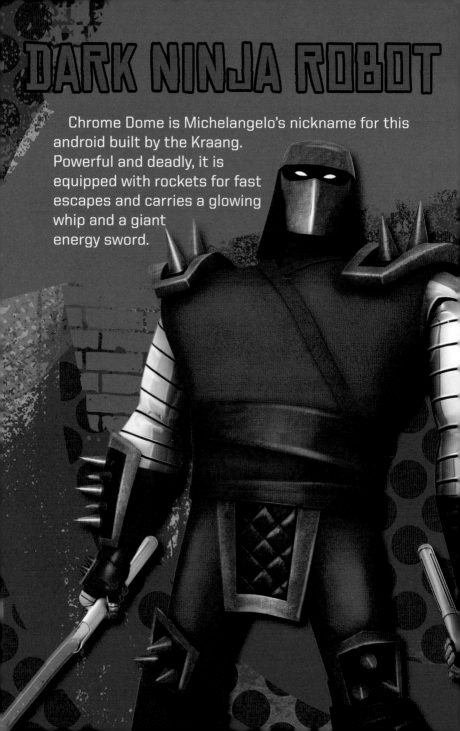

had bested Karai once again. As April stood safely away from the action, Karai was on the ground, staring down the razor-sharp end of Leo's *katana*.

"It's over, Karai," he said.

"For now!" she replied, throwing down a ninja smoke bomb. In a flash, the Shredder's evil daughter disappeared. When the dust settled, it was the Turtles—and their best friend, April—who were left standing.

Together.

This was cause for celebration. But Mikey didn't realize it. He was still too entranced by the awesomeness of the plasma sword. He pulled the glowing blade from Chrome Dome's back and studied it. "Can I keep it? Can I keep it?" he begged.

April smiled. It felt good to have her friends back. But it also felt like her entire body was going to be bruised tomorrow.

"That . . . wasn't . . . too difficult," she wheezed as Leo helped her up.

"Easy does it," he told her. "It's over now."

"I just need to catch my breath."

Donnie, Raph, and Mikey joined them.

"Thanks, guys," April said to them with a smile. "I just wanted to say . . ."

But she trailed off, her eyes widening in panic. The Turtles were confused. *Just wanted to say what?*

And with a gasp, April remembered, blurting out: "Oh, my gosh! I forgot about Casey!"

April raced out of the park toward the hockey rink.

Donnie just sighed. *"That's* what she wanted to say?"

April threw open the doors to the hockey rink, her mind reeling. Was Casey okay? Was he hurt?

To her surprise, he was just fine. In fact, he seemed to be having the time of his life, finishing off a Footbot with his stick.

"That is how you play hockey!" Casey said, standing victorious over a pile of Footbots.

"Casey! Are you okay?" April cried, running out onto the ice without any skates, slipping and sliding.

"Of course I am," he said, catching her in his arms. "Steady there, Red."

He held her close, her heart beating fast. They smiled, staring into each other's eyes. In that moment neither of them had to say a word. They both felt it—they were going to be more than just study partners.

Casey had never seen April so happy.

And neither had Donnie.

He was secretly watching them from the stands. Even though he had April back, her heart belonged to someone else.

CHAPTER 14

The next day, April made her way below the surface. It had been months since she visited the Turtles' lair. In a way, it felt like she was returning home. She got butterflies in her stomach when she glimpsed them in their natural habitat again: four mutant brothers gathered around the TV, watching some weird anime show together.

Like a family.

Her family.

"Hey, guys," she said, surprising them.

One by one, the Turtles looked up from the TV set. They were all smiles.

"April!"

"You're back!"

"What's up?"

Even Master Splinter broke meditation to come out and welcome her back to the *dojo* after a long time away. "It is very good to see you, April."

"I missed you, Master Splinter. I hope we can start training again soon."

"Of course," Splinter replied. "Whenever you wish."

She respectfully bowed to her former sensei before turning back to the Turtles. She paused, shifting uneasily. "I never got a chance to tell you guys that I'm sorry . . . for everything."

"*You're* sorry?" Leo replied, remembering the events of that fateful night.

The mutagen.

The accident.

Her father.

"But *we* were the ones who screwed up," Leo continued apologetically.

"It was an accident," April said, speaking from the heart. "And more importantly, you're my friends. I don't ever want to hold a grudge again."

"You're the best, April!" Mikey said, offering her a slice of pizza. "To mark this day, I offer you . . . the Slice of Eternal Reunion."

April looked the slice up and down. What had once been a scrumptious slice of cheese pizza had become a science project. "It has lint and dead bugs all over it."

"I know. I just found it under my bed," Mikey explained, cradling it like some priceless relic. "It's . . . eternal."

Realizing April wasn't going to touch the slice, Mikey decided to honor it the best way he knew how: by scarfing it down in one bite!

April stepped around the others and walked up to Donnie. The closer she got, the faster his heart beat. She locked eyes with him. "Thanks for always being there . . . even when I didn't want you to be."

She threw her arms around him.

And as if the moment couldn't get any better, April gave Donnie a tiny kiss on the cheek.

Donnie felt a rush unlike any he'd ever felt before. Forget defeating Shredder and the Technodrome. Today was now officially the best day of his life. He stared at her with hearts in his eyes and only one thought on his mind: *I love being a Turtle!*

Mutant monsters and robot ninjas are takin' over my city.

How long before those freaks hurt somebody close to me?

Like my dad.

Or my little sister.

Or April.

I'm not waitin' around to find out.

All my life I've known that I'm meant for something greater.

This is my calling.

My destiny.

A true warrior has gotta be prepared.

CHAPTER 15

Casey barely recognized his face in the mirror.

Since his battle with the Footbots, he'd decided to make some changes. He'd upped his workout—chin-ups, push-ups, you name it—and bulked up as much as he could. He needed to be stronger than ever. He needed to be able to take a beating. He needed to be ready for *combat*.

Next, he suited up for battle. He started with his hockey pads. Normal gloves were great on the ice, but for hero work, they needed a little something extra. With some industrial glue, he added rusty nails to his blocker, and voila! Homemade spiked gauntlets.

Then he focused on his weapons. He taped up

his old hockey sticks and stuck them in a sheath, which he slung across his back. There was room for more, so he added a baseball bat and an old golf club he found in a Dumpster to his arsenal. Those felt right. But deep down, he knew that to compete with robots and monsters and other weirdoes who had high-tech weaponry, he needed more of an edge. So he borrowed a potato masher from the kitchen and hooked it up to some old batteries to make his very own electroshock weapon.

Casey studied himself in the mirror and practiced his trash talk. "Who do you think you are?" he asked the imaginary villains all around him. "A ninja?"

He tested his electroshock weapon. It crackled with tendrils of electricity. He was pleased with the *shocking* results.

"Bring it, punk!" he said, trying his best to sound tough.

Perfect. Now for the finishing touch, he thought.

He needed to look menacing. He needed to harness fear and mold it into a mask. A face that would send a chill up the spines of bad guys everywhere.

And suddenly it hit him.

A goalie's mask.

He blew most of his money on spray paint at the local art store. Enough to give his mask a fearsome facelift. He toyed with many different designs and finally landed on one that felt bad . . . to the *bone*.

A skull.

He covered it with glow-white spray paint.

Then he put it on, checking out his new look in the mirror.

He didn't look like a kid anymore. He looked just as freaky as those mutant monsters waiting out there for him. He was a dangerous creature now, a force to be reckoned with.

"Scum-suckin' mutated freaks of the world, prepare to meet . . . CASEY JONES."

CHAPTER 16

Casey Jones wasn't the only one preparing for a fight. So were the Turtles.

As part of a new training exercise, Master Splinter had them report to the *dojo* with their weapons ready. The wise sensei stood before them with a solemn air until he had complete silence.

"My sons," he said, admiring their flawless form, "you are truly becoming impressive warriors. But to grow as a team, you must know each other's strengths and weaknesses."

At that moment, Mikey broke his silence—by unleashing the smelliest burp ever! The fumes were so strong they wafted to Donnie's nostrils and refused to let go.

"Right in my face?" Donnie gagged. "Really?"

"Garlic and clam pizza," Mikey said with confidence.

Splinter ignored this. "This competition is a free-for-all. Last Turtle standing wins!" he announced, then gave the Japanese command to begin: *"Hajime!"*

"I'm still seeing spots," Donnie mumbled. Mikey's burp fumes had clouded his vision, which Raph used to his advantage. He snuck up behind Donnie and roundhouse-kicked him into the tree!

"Sorry, Donnie," he said with a smirk. "It's a ninja-eat-ninja world!"

Raph got his *sais* ready for his next victim: Mikey. He chased his little brother around the *dojo,* hoping to catch him off guard. He saw his opportunity.

Until Leo jumped in his way.

Sparks flew as their blades met—Leo's *katanas* clashing against the cold steel of Raph's *sais.*

"What are you doing, Leo?" Raph growled. "I was goin' for Mikey!"

"What part of 'last Turtle standing' don't you understand?" Leo fired back. He shoved Raph, opening a clear lane to Mikey. Leo slid down the middle of the room and took out Mikey with one leg sweep!

"Aw, man!" Mikey yelped.

The score was even: Raph 1, Leo 1.

"Looks like you leveled up to the boss fight," Raph taunted.

"I'm gonna wipe that smirk off your face . . . *permanently,*" Leo replied.

A hush fell over the *dojo* again. Donnie, Mikey, and Splinter all watched the face-off with intense anticipation. It was clear Leo and Raph were the two strongest fighters. But considering their advanced skills, shared fearlessness, and equal strength and speed, neither Turtle had a clear edge.

Each punch met with another punch. A block with a block.

It wasn't until they began to disarm each other that things got interesting. To the untrained eye, it looked like Raph had Leo on the run, forcing him toward the tree in the center of the room. But Mikey and Donnie knew better; Leo was setting

himself up to gain the higher ground in the fight.

And once Raph ducked behind the tree, using it as a shield against Leo's oncoming strikes, Leo knew he had him. He ran up the branches, propelling himself into the air for an epic windmill kick! His foot clocked Raph right in the jaw, sending him skidding along the floor.

Leo was the last Turtle standing.

Raph opened his eyes to see Leo bowing victoriously before Master Splinter. He could feel the anger well up in his throat. He couldn't believe he'd lost.

"Leo won it this time!" Donnie called out, which sent Raph over the edge. He picked himself up and growled, a blind rage overtaking him.

"Uh-oh," Mikey warned, sensing that Raph was about to explode. "He's awoken the *beast*!"

Raph charged forward and sucker-punched Leo right in the face!

Leo dropped like a cold fish to the *dojo* floor.

Donnie and Mikey immediately ran over. "Raph! What are you doing?"

Hearing the disappointment in Donnie's voice,

Raph snapped back into reality. "I—I—I didn't mean to hurt him!" he stammered in a panic. He looked from Leo's limp body to Master Splinter's disapproving eyes. "It was an accident. Seriously!"

Leo slowly awoke. He sat up, the world coming into focus again. Nursing his throbbing head, he said, "Did anyone get the number of that bus?"

"We have spoken about this time and again, Raphael," Master Splinter scolded. "Anger is a dangerous ally. It clouds your judgment. You need to control it, lest it control you."

"But, Sensei, I wasn't angry. I was just *determined* to win."

Raph saw the way his brothers were looking at him. He knew that look. He had messed up. He had crossed a line. And there was nothing he could do or say to make it better.

Which made him angry all over again.

"WHAT?" Raph shouted at them, enraged. "I said I WASN'T angry!"

But they knew that wasn't true. And so did he.

Raph stormed out of the sewers, angrier than ever.

Raph hit the surface to try and cool off, but it was no use.

"This always happens!" he screamed. "I'm fine until those guys push my buttons!"

His temper was running hot, and the only thing that was going to make him feel better was to hit someone. Or something. *Anything.* So he went on a rampage, knocking over garbage cans, pummeling mailboxes, and even punching the air. Nothing was safe from his rage.

"It's not like I was trying to hurt Leo," he confessed to the night. It was a pity no one was around to hear his side of the story. He took a deep breath. Saying it out loud felt good. He was finally calming down.

"They just don't get it," he sighed.

From a fire escape ten stories high, Casey Jones could see everything. He was a crime fighter now. It was up to him to protect this great city he called home.

He took out his journal, chronicling another night on patrol:

My city is infested. A boil. A festering sore. It stinks with evil. Pure evil that only Casey Jones can face.

Casey smiled. That sounded good. Unfortunately, it was far from the truth. Over the past few nights, nothing had happened. No monsters. No mutants. No old ladies who needed help crossing the street. The city was quieter than the school library.

"Actually . . . crime fighting's pretty boring," he admitted.

Then Casey sensed something moving in the shadows behind him. It scurried toward him with

amazing speed! *"Yaaaaahhhh!!!"* he shrieked, scurrying to get away from it.

A rat. Nothing but a rat.

Casey saw the pest and shuddered. He could deal with villains of any size, but rats? *Ewwwww!* They carried diseases and smelled like a toilet. They were his only weakness.

"I hate those furry little freaks!" he said.

That was it. Casey had had enough for tonight. He sheathed his hockey sticks and was about to pack it in, when he heard a commotion coming from the alleyway below.

Is someone in trouble?

Casey ducked, watching a street gang rough up a harmless old man.

The Purple Dragons—the meanest gang on the East Side. Those guys were the worst. They took the old man's money.

Casey saw a glint of steel—one of the gang members had a knife.

Casey pulled his mask over his face. It seemed his hockey sticks would see some action after all.

Sid, the most muscle-bound member of the Purple Dragons, laughed at the old man. "Get his watch, too!" he told the other gang members with a chuckle. He thought mugging people was hilarious.

What he did not find funny, however, was being knocked to the ground unexpectedly. Sid found himself lying on the concrete, shooting pains throbbing through his skull. He picked up the strange circular object that had nailed him.

A hockey puck? "What the—"

Sid stopped short. He couldn't believe what he saw standing before him—a deranged hockey player!

"You slimeballs picked the wrong night," the

demonic skull-face growled from the darkness.

"Nice outfit," another Purple Dragon sneered. "Who's this clown?"

Casey Jones stepped out of the shadows. "I'm the last guy you see before you wake up in the hospital."

With that, Casey gave the Purple Dragons a fight they'd never forget. Wielding his hockey stick, he swatted, jabbed, and struck the gang members down until they were crumpled on the ground and begging for mercy.

If this had been on the ice, he'd have about two dozen penalties, but on the street, this was a just comeuppance for a gang that had terrorized the city for too long. And it was being watched from afar by a mysterious figure perched high on the rooftops—Raphael.

Part of him enjoyed seeing the Purple Dragons get creamed in a fight, but he knew this masked vigilante was going too far. "That guy's out of control," Raph said, spinning his *sais*. "Time for a little intervention."

CHAPTER 19

Casey teed up another puck, aiming squarely at the Purple Dragons. He called his own play-by-play once again: "Casey Jones shoots—"

One of the thugs took off toward traffic. Casey whacked the puck with all his strength, nailing the moving target in the back of the head.

"And he scores!" Casey celebrated.

"Hey, man . . . enough!" Sid pleaded, wincing from the pain. "We give up!"

But Casey ignored him. These thugs needed to be taught a lesson, and going easy on them was not an option. Besides, did they go easy on the innocent people they mugged and beat up daily? No.

"I ain't finished with you lowlifes yet," Casey

told him, prepping his hockey stick for another hit.

Raph dropped into their midst, undetected by Casey Jones. He snuck up and swiped Casey's hockey stick, then quickly disappeared into the shadows.

"What the—?!" Casey gasped, realizing his hands were empty. He looked around but couldn't see anyone else. So he reached for his backup weapon: a baseball bat. "Who's back there? Show yourself!"

The Turtles didn't like to reveal themselves to humans, but Raph knew there was no other way. So he took a breath and emerged from the darkness.

"Another mutant?"

"Got a problem with that?" Raph said, and gnashed his teeth.

"Wait. What are you? Like some kinda . . . *turtle ninja?*" Casey busted out laughing.

Raph fought to keep calm, but this masked maniac was really steaming his shell!

Casey kept chuckling, and the Purple Dragons saw their opportunity to sneak away. They took off running.

"Hey, you filthy scum, I'm not done with you!"

Casey yelled, about to pursue them—when he felt the turtle's hand holding him back.

"Let me handle this," Raph said.

Casey shoved him. "Outta my way!"

Raph was incensed. There was no reasoning with this hockey hothead. All he seemed to understand was pure rage. Now Raph knew how his brothers must have felt when they had to deal with his temper tantrums.

"You know, anger is a dangerous ally," Raph said, quoting Master Splinter. Funny—when Splinter said it, it sounded so calm. But Raph was irked. And coming from him, it sounded less like friendly advice and more like a threat.

"So why don't you cool off for a while?" he added, shoving Casey back. Hard.

"That's it, lizard. I'm done with you." Casey roared. He charged at Raph, belting out his signature war cry: "GOONGALAAAA!!!"

He slashed at the turtle in a fury of spinning thrusts and wild haymaker punches. But Raph was too quick for him.

Raph caught Casey's stick with his *sais,* artfully throwing him off balance. "I told you, back off!"

And just when Casey was about to retaliate, Raph delivered a spin kick to his chest. It sent Casey hurtling backward into a Dumpster, the wind knocked out of his lungs. Casey Jones didn't know the meaning of the word *quit.*

Time for round two.

Casey shook off the garbage and climbed out of the Dumpster. "You let those muggers go," he said, breathing heavily. "You're gonna pay for that, *freak.*"

Casey lowered his shoulder and barreled into Raph, pinning his shell against a wall. He grabbed the handle of his best slugger.

Raph lunged forward, ducking the bat, which connected with the brick wall instead of his face! He somersaulted over Casey Jones, flinging ninja stars along the way.

Casey smiled at the steely ninja stars sticking out of his hockey pads. He'd only seen those in old kung fu movies! He paused. "Gotta admit, throwing stars are cool."

"Then let me show you my *sais*!" Raph said.

Raph unleashed a *kata* combo of savage *sai* strikes and power kicks. And yet somehow, Casey held him off—with nothing but his store-bought baseball bat and an old hockey stick. He fought with heart. Amid the chaos of battle, even Raph could acknowledge the kid's fearlessness.

They continued trading lunges until—

THWACK!

Raphael booted Casey in the jaw in a flawless aerial move before landing gracefully.

The hockey punk was seeing stars.

Raph relaxed for a second.

Casey looked up at him with anger and admiration. This wasn't over. He collected his hockey stick and rose to his feet.

This Turtle had some secret weapons, but so did he.

With a click, Casey released his spiked skates. Custom in-line wheels appeared from his soles. Razor-sharp blades glistened at the toes.

Let's see the lizard keep up with me now, Casey

thought. He skated out of the alleyway, luring Raph into the street.

Raph was fuming. Once he got his hands on Casey, he'd rip him limb from limb . . . if he could catch him! On wheels, Casey was way too fast! He skated circles around Raph. He rolled over parked cars, smacking Raph with his hockey stick every time he came around.

Once on his head!

Another on his shell!

And a third to the jaw! There was no way of stopping this spinning skate-storm of doom! All Raph could see was a revolving blur around him.

He could feel his anger bubbling up in his throat.

First his brothers push him too far.

Now this kid pushes him down to the ground?

Casey skated forward to finish him off, but Raph—rage coursing through him—recovered in time to grab Casey's hockey stick and rip it away. He rolled upright and pinned Casey against the hood of a car. He grabbed him by his hockey pads and slammed his head down with a painful thud.

"Ugh!" Casey wheezed. "That hurt!"

In a legendary fury, Raph roared. He put his foot down on Casey's throat, and raised his *sai* in the air.

He brought the blade down.

And Casey Jones screamed—until he realized he was okay. Nothing happened.

Raph couldn't do it.

"What am I doing? Maybe I do have anger issues," Raph said, talking himself down. As he sheathed his *sais* and loosened his grip, the petrified Casey saw a way out.

He flicked his wrist, releasing a crackling bolt of electricity from underneath his arm pads.

The homemade electroshock weapon!

A few thousand volts dropped Raph to his knees. He tumbled backward, nearly getting hit by a car in the process. He spun to dodge it, and when he turned back, Casey was already down the street—holding on to the bumper of a taxicab, skitching away to freedom.

"You ain't seen the last of me, Turtle!" Raph heard Casey yell before disappearing around the corner.

CHAPTER 20

April couldn't believe her eyes: Casey Jones was actually in school! He had become a rare sight around Roosevelt High lately.

April and her friend Irma walked up behind him. April was excited to see him after he'd missed their last few study sessions. "Well, well," she said with a smile. "Casey Jones finally makes it to class! What a surprise! Ready for the big trig exam today?"

"Trig exam?" he mumbled into his locker. "Oh yeah . . ."

Casey didn't turn around to talk to her as he normally would. It seemed like he was trying to hide something.

"I was up all night," he said, finally turning around. "Studying . . ."

April gasped. Casey's face was a swollen mess, completely covered in purple-and-black bruises!

"Really? Did your homework punch you in the face?" she asked.

Casey tried to cover. But the only thing he could come up with was "I had . . . uhhh . . . last-minute hockey practice."

"I thought the rink was closed after dark, ever since that mysterious fight broke out there a few weeks back," Irma said, butting into their conversation. She pushed her glasses up, leaning in to take a closer look at Casey's injuries. "So how exactly did you get those bruises, Casey? Huh?"

"What are you, Irma, my interrogator?"

Irma rolled her eyes at him, walking back to class. She tried to pull April along with her, but Casey managed to steal her for a quick moment.

"I saw something crazy last night," he whispered to her. "A mutant."

A dark look fell over April's face.

"C'mon, April," she heard Irma nag from down the hall. "We've got our exam, and I will not be late this time!"

Casey and April shared an apprehensive look. He desperately wanted to explain his whole bizarre night to her. But it was too late. . . . April was already off to class.

The popcorn was popped, and the guys were ready to settle in for a butt-numbing marathon of their favorite TV show. Donnie got comfy in his spot on the couch, until Mikey cannonballed into the cushion next to him, sending popcorn everywhere!

"Yo!" Mikey yelled. "You ready for forty-eight hours of evil-fightin', galaxy-savin', super action?!"

"I *was* . . . until you spilled greasy popcorn ALL OVER ME!" Donnie cried.

"My bad," Mikey replied. He decided to do the decent, and delicious, thing: he picked the kernels off Donnie's face one by one—and ate them.

While Mikey was busy cleaning up his mess,

Raph pulled Leo aside. "You got a minute?" he asked.

Leo sighed. "Well, I was gonna watch *Super Robo Mecha Force*—"

"Cool, so . . . ," Raph awkwardly began. "Here's the deal. See . . . I . . . me . . ."

Leo was taken aback. He'd never seen Raph struggle like this before!

"Sorry," Raph finally whispered.

Leo couldn't believe it. Raph *never* apologized. This was a first in Turtle history, and he knew he had to make this moment last.

"What was that?" Leo asked, pretending not to have heard him.

"I said I was . . . sorry."

Leo cupped his ear, pretending to strain to hear the words.

"Sorry! Okay? SORRY!" Raph blurted out.

Everyone heard it that time. Donnie's and Mikey's mouths dropped open at the announcement.

"I thought I had my anger under control," Raph confessed. "Turns out I didn't. But now I do! Seriously."

"He means for now," Mikey called out from the couch, butting in. "I give him ten more seconds." And then, still munching his popcorn, he started the countdown: "Nine . . . eight . . . seven . . ."

With that, Raph could feel his blood pressure shoot up like a rocket. He bit his lip.

"What are you saying, Raph?" Leo prodded, sensing his brother's anger was being triggered. "It's not that you are angry, but we *make* you angry?"

Mikey kept counting: "Six . . . five . . . four . . . three . . . two . . . one—"

"SHUT UP!" Raph yelled in a rage.

"Bing-bing-bing!" Mikey joked. "We have a winner!"

Raph was panting short breaths, trying to keep his cool. But it was too late for that now. His brothers didn't have any faith in him. And that really got him steamed! He shrugged Leo away and started to walk out of the sewer.

Again.

"Raph, wait! I was just busting your shell," Leo explained.

Donnie had had enough of his moody older brother for one evening. "Eh, let the big green baby go."

Raph flung a ninja star toward his brothers, puncturing the popcorn bag. Kernels exploded all over the place.

Raph punched his way out of the sewer, the manhole cover flying off into the street.

"Those guys are making me loopy!" he fumed, kicking the air. "They just don't get me!"

Raph leaped on top of a nearby Dumpster and scaled a fire escape toward the sky above. He wanted to get as far away from his brothers as possible.

CHAPTER 22

At that moment, high atop a different building, Casey Jones was scribbling in his journal. He'd been busy working on a cartoon that perfectly captured his battle with the turtle ninja. As he shaded in the details on his drawing, he winced at the soreness from their fight.

It's been three days and my body still feels like a punching bag, he thought, conscious of the dull ache he felt underneath his hockey gear. *That*

turtle's a worthy opponent, I'll give him that. He sketched the turtle's face carefully, its odd look still fresh in his mind. There was something different about this turtle ninja. Something almost . . . *human*. It wasn't a blank slate like those robo-ninjas from the rink. And it wasn't a mindless creature like the goo monster. It was unique.

A flash of green caught Casey's attention. He looked up from the page.

The turtle was practicing its ninja moves on the rooftop of an adjacent building.

Casey put his journal away, grabbed his hockey sticks, and headed toward it, unaware that he'd been under surveillance the entire time.

A spindly Footbot waited for Casey to disappear down to the street before it crept out of the darkness. It chirped, sending a homing signal back to its master.

CHAPTER 23

Tracking the turtle ninja was easy. All Casey had to do was follow the sounds of crashing Dumpsters and shrieking alley cats across the city. The turtle ninja was obviously angry, punching everything in its path. It even stopped to babble to itself!

"Anger issues? Who's got anger issues? I don't have anger issues! Maybe *they* have anger issues!" he heard the turtle say as it tore up a manhole cover and dropped down into the sewers.

Casey followed carefully. His eyes adjusted to the darkness in time for him to see the turtle make a sharp turn to the left.

He was so focused on tailing the turtle that

he didn't notice the pitter-patter of footsteps in the puddles behind him.

A swarm of Footbots was shadowing his every move.

Leo, Donnie, and Mikey hadn't moved a muscle since Raph left. They were all in a relaxed haze in front of the TV, still binge-watching *Super Robo Mecha Force Five.* It was an action-packed episode where the bad guy surprised the heroes with a sneak attack in their very own base!

Leo scoffed at this. "C'mon, how can one guy infiltrate Super Robo Mecha headquarters?"

As Mikey prepared an elaborately geeky answer for him, they heard Raph step back into the lair.

"You guys watch so much TV, your brains are gonna rot," Raph said.

"Yay, Raph's back," Donnie replied in an intentional monotone.

Raph sighed, doing his best to ignore the negativity and remain as calm as possible.

"You cool off yet, man?" Leo asked him.

"I'm always cool," Raph said, trying to fit on the couch. "Move over."

Casey finally caught up to him, stealthily moving through the shadows. He glanced around the room, and his eyes instantly widened at the incredible sight before him—a whole group of turtle ninjas! He gasped in amazement. *There are four of them?*

Casey crouched for a closer look and accidentally knocked over some leftover pizza boxes and a fork, which clanged loudly on the floor.

He was busted.

"Intruder!" Donnie screamed.

The Turtles spun around to see the masked man standing in their living room.

"Awww, man!" Casey whined.

The Turtles bolted up from the couch and rushed Casey all at once. They held him down before he could get away.

Raph recognized the hockey psycho from the other night. "*YOU* again!"

"You know this guy, Raph?" Mikey asked.

"Get your stinkin' paws off me!" Casey growled.

When Leo ripped Casey's skull mask off, they all bugged out. The man underneath was a skeletal, decaying mess! Pockets of black goo made his eyes seem sunken in, like a zombie's. And his freakishly long grin framed a ghost-white face.

Leo leaned in for a closer look, hesitating. Then, he lowered his guard. "It's face paint," he realized. "He's just a kid!"

"Let go of me, you stupid reptiles!" Casey demanded. "Let go!"

From the other side of the room, two new voices rose above the commotion. "Always trust your instincts. A well-honed intuition can be sharper than your eyes," said one.

"Yes, Sensei," replied a very familiar and much softer voice.

Casey was confused. *It couldn't be. There's no way. Why would she . . . ?*

He turned. He saw April running toward him.

"Casey? Casey!" she yelled, panicked.

With that, everyone froze.

"You know this guy?" the Turtles asked her.

"You know these guys?" Casey said, totally confounded.

The Turtles loosened their grip. April pushed through and stood between them and Casey. "Don't hurt him," she begged them. "He's my friend!"

April gave him a look. "Casey, what are you doing here?"

Casey didn't know what to think. "A better question is: how do you know these . . . *freaks*?"

"These are the other friends I told you about."

"Wait," Casey said, slowly wrapping his head around the situation. "So they're *not* the bad guys?"

"No way!" April sighed. She'd known this day would come eventually. She just hadn't thought it would come so soon. Her two worlds were about to collide. "Casey Jones, meet Leonardo, Donatello, Michelangelo . . ."

"What up?" Mikey said, just as Raph slapped him upside the head.

"And the one and only Raphael," April said with a wave of her hand.

Casey took a breath, looking around the semi-circle of green faces staring back at him. In a world where he could fight mutants and monsters and robots, maybe Red's knowing a whole clan of turtle ninjas wasn't shocking after all. But he had a question.

"So," he asked, "the Turtles are all Italian?"

"No," came the answer from behind him. "I named them after my favorite painters and sculptors of the Italian Renaissance."

The owner of the voice stepped into the light,

fully revealing his furry face. It was a giant rat dressed in samurai robes!

A terrified look fell over Casey's face. He could feel his knees weakening. Regular mutants he could handle, but mutant rats that knew how to speak English? He started to feel dizzy.

"Casey?" April said, sensing something was wrong.

Casey's eyes rolled back in his head and he fainted.

April rushed over. "Casey? Casey! Wake up!"

After a few moments of unconsciousness and a helpful slap to the face, April finally got Casey to wake up.

"This is Master Splinter," April explained to him. "He's cool."

"You do not have to fear me, my friend. Rest assured, I do not bite," Master Splinter promised.

"He's a giant . . . talking . . . RAT!" Casey stammered.

Raph burst out laughing. "Big bad vigilante's afraid of rats!"

At that moment, Mikey held a cockroach up to Raph's ear, which made him fully retract into his shell!

Mikey chuckled. "Just like you and cockroaches. Huh, Raph?"

While everyone shared a laugh at Raph, April frowned and held her head as if something was wrong. She hadn't gotten one of these feelings in a long while, but there was no denying it. Her psychic signal was strong, and at that very moment, she was sensing that something bad was in their midst.

"What is it, April?" Master Splinter asked.

"Sensei," she replied, suddenly compelled to look up at the ceiling, "we are not alone."

Everyone followed her gaze upward . . . to see a mass of Footbots! The Turtles' lair was infested!

CHAPTER 24

The Turtles were outnumbered.

Even with Casey picking up the rear, they were only seven against a swarm of what seemed like a hundred Footbots—their spindly arms extending with all types of chain saws and weapons at their disposal.

The Turtles found themselves sweating with their shells against the wall. Their home was now a battleground, and in Leo's mind, there was only one Turtle to blame. "Raph!" he said, his eyes narrowing into an accusatory glare. "*You* led the enemy right to our lair!"

"It's the kid's fault!" Raph insisted, gesturing toward Casey. "He was following me!"

Casey gasped. He was only trying to get a closer look at the mysterious Turtle, not get everyone killed! "My fault?"

Unlike his brothers, Mikey didn't really care whose fault it was. All he knew was that they had to protect the lair. The time for talking was over. *"Booyakasha!"* he yelled, charging the Footbots with his *nunchucks* spinning.

CLUNK! CLUNK!

Mikey took out two Footbots on his own before the other Turtles jumped in to back him up. Leo was right there to slice and dice his way through a few oncoming bots while Donnie pinned the next wave down with nothing but his secret *bo* staff blade.

Even Master Splinter and April got in on the action! With a barrage of well-practiced power punches and throwing moves, the teacher/student duo knocked off a few of the Footbots' heads, teaching them a very painful lesson!

Now it was Raph's turn. He leaped into the center of the room—and felt someone at his back, fighting along with him. He turned to look, expecting to see one of his brothers. Only it wasn't a Turtle!

It was Casey Jones!

Raph scoffed. *What does this kid think he's doing?*

"You're the one who did this," Raph said, clobbering a few Footbots mid-sentence.

WHAM!

"They followed you, too, dude!" Casey insisted, perfectly happy to fight off a few bots while he argued his side.

THWACK!

"Don't *dude* me, dude!"

And while the two frenemies continued to bicker and fight off bots simultaneously, Master Splinter picked up the slack. With lightning-fast speed and expert-level *ninjutsu* moves, the ninja master moved quicker than the human eye could see. He single-handedly chopped, kicked, and tail-whipped his way through ten Footbots until they were nothing but a pile of metal limbs.

"Stay alert! More are coming!" Master Splinter warned, spotting a freshly spawned group of Footbots headed their way.

Donnie noticed one Footbot standing still, its head mysteriously swiveling left to right. Its eyes glowed red. Was it powering up? Taking surveillance photos?

It took Donnie a moment, but he soon realized what was happening. That Footbot was trying to transmit a homing signal!

"He'll give away our location!" Donnie cried.

"Don't let that robot escape!" Master Splinter commanded.

A voice piped up behind him. "Casey Jones is on it!"

Determined to make things right, Casey sprinted after the Footbot—just as someone sideswiped him, knocking him out of the way.

Raph!

"Tell Casey Jones I don't need his help!" he said.

Raph left Casey in the dust. If anyone was going to save the lair, it was going to be him!

CHAPTER 25

Raph chased the Footbot through the city's underground tunnels. But he wasn't the only one.

Casey Jones was right there with him, keeping pace a few steps ahead. Even under all those heavy hockey pads, he was fast! Raph removed a grappling hook from his shell and swung it around like a lasso, taking aim.

The hook connected—direct hit—and wrapped around Casey, pulling him to the ground.

"What are you doing?!" Casey scowled.

"Me?" Raph said, taking the lead. "You got in my way!"

Casey wriggled out of the ropes, scrambling back to his feet. He saw Raph's shell up ahead in

the distance and broke into a full-on sprint. Under-
foot, he noticed the ground gradually change from
rocky puddles to gravel and train tracks.

They weren't in the sewers anymore. They
were in the subway.

Raph paused. The Footbot disappeared into
the darkness of the tunnels.

Casey finally caught up. "Where'd he go?"

A group of shadowy figures suddenly landed
all around them.

More Footbots! It was an ambush!

Now Raph had no choice but to fight along-
side Casey Jones, and he was not happy about it.
They joined forces, brawling together—Raph with
his *sais,* Casey with his sticks—making quick work
of the robot attack squad.

"If that Transmitter Footbot gets back to
Karai and gives away our hideout, you answer to
Splinter!" Raph threatened between lunges.

"The rat?" Casey shuddered. He did not want
to face those whiskers. He needed to think of
something fast.

As if on cue, a second wave of Footbots emerged from the shadows. Since all the robots looked the same, tracking the Transmitter Footbot wasn't going to be easy in this crowd of identical black masks.

Then he spotted two glowing red eyes in the back of the shadowy crowd. The Transmitter Footbot!

That's it, Casey thought. *Color.* He knew what he needed to do. He pulled a homemade graffiti grenade from his belt and bit off the cap. He took careful aim, gave it a shake, and flung the spray-paint can into the cloaked masses.

Casey saw an explosion of gold liquid. He'd hit it! The Transmitter Footbot was marked with Casey's paint!

But there was no time to celebrate. The Transmitter Footbot was getting away!

"Next time, tag it with a *real* grenade!" Raph said with a smirk.

The two unlikely allies took off after their moving target. Side by side.

CHAPTER 26

Meanwhile, back at the lair, the other Turtles had Footbot problems of their own. The pesky robots had infiltrated Donnie's lab and were threatening to trash everything, from Donnie's new Turtle-tech prototypes to the contraband Kraang devices they'd spent months recovering.

Mikey fended off a few Footbots and leaped on top of a rolling toolbox. He pushed off it, using it like a battering ram on wheels. He took out a few bots with finesse—until he accidentally crashed into a table of explosive chemicals.

KABOOM!

The purple flash of the explosion illuminated the room.

"Stop messin' around!" Donnie scolded. "You'll blow us all to Philadelphia!"

Mikey blushed. "Sorry, D!"

Casey Jones skated along the train tracks, desperately trying to catch the Transmitter Footbot before it could reach the surface. He looked over his shoulder and saw Raph struggling to keep up. "Faster, man! Move your shell!"

They both heard a rumbling sound. A subway train was barreling toward them, flying like a silver bullet out of the darkness.

Casey started to freak. If they didn't move, they'd be pancaked for sure!

With the train right at his back, Casey slowed down and dove, tackling Raph. They rolled away from the tracks and down the gravel banks. The wind of the passing train roared around them.

Raph opened his eyes . . . and saw Casey Jones standing over him. They were safe.

"You okay?" Casey asked.

Raph breathed a sigh of relief. The kid had saved his life. Maybe he wasn't such a bad guy after all. "Yeah, thanks."

Raph exhaled and then remembered: the Transmitter Footbot!

The shifty bot had scaled the moving subway cars and climbed on top of them, hitching a high-speed ride through the tunnels.

Raph put his issues with Casey aside and shook off whatever pent-up anger he had left. He gave Casey a friendly look, as if to say, *Shall we?*

Understanding that Raph would hop a moving train just to smash a robo-ninja—and was inviting him along for the ride—Casey knew he'd found a new, true friend.

It was time to catch a train.

CHAPTER 27

On top of the speeding train, hot, stinky wind whipped against Casey's and Raph's faces. They spotted the Transmitter Footbot dragging itself from car to car with its four mechanical arms outstretched. The bot stopped and looked back at them.

Battling to stay balanced on the train, Casey and Raph lumbered forward and drew their weapons. They'd come this far. They were ready to shut this thing down for good.

But they weren't ready for what happened next: the Transmitter Footbot released its grip from the train-top and let the wind get underneath it. The blast carried the bot straight at Raph and Casey.

They ducked, dodging its airborne chain saws.

The Transmitter Footbot grabbed hold of the top of the train once more, catching itself before it could fly off the back end. It extended its blades and clawed toward them for another attack.

Raph darted out of the way, barely holding on. Casey lurched forward, swinging his hockey stick, but the force of the train caused him to lose his footing.

Raph saw him disappear off the side and threw his grappling hook expertly. The rope caught Casey just in time! He dangled inches above the rushing tracks.

Raph hauled Casey up, grabbing his partner's hand to help him back onto the train's roof.

"Thanks, Raph," Casey said.

"Now we're even," Raph replied.

Raph and Casey fought the wind, stomping toward their target with determination. The bot had made its way to the front of the train. A station overpass, an enclosed walkway with big windows, loomed ahead. This was the bot's chance to escape to the surface.

As the nose of the train crossed under the walk-way, the Transmitter Footbot vaulted itself upward, crashing through a window.

Casey wasn't going to lose him. He launched himself, and the momentum of the train carried him into the overpass. Casey landed on his feet and immediately started swinging. The bot dodged this way and that to avoid Casey's swinging baseball bat.

Raph stormed in, bumping into Casey because the hall was so narrow. Ticked that he didn't have enough room to move around and hit the bot, he yelled at Casey: "Outta my way!"

The Footbot broke free, trying to make a run for it, when Casey lashed out with his last hockey stick. He was too wide again!

Raph rolled forward and kicked the Foot-bot hard in its metal midsection, its spindly body clanging down the stairs and into an abandoned subway station.

Not one to be outdone, Casey snuck around Raph, grinding down the stairwell rail on his

skates. "I can take this robot down myself!"

Raph smirked. Seemed like all the friendly courtesies were out the window when it came to who would be first to wreck the robot. *May the best man—or* Turtle—*win!*

Casey chased the bot through the turnstiles, and Raph somersaulted in a few feet away. He threw his *sai* at it and—

THA-CLUNK!

The blade pierced the Footbot's shoulder, pinning it to a pillar. It quickly pulled itself free, its circuits still sparking from the hit, and bolted toward the main exit stairwell.

"It's going for the street!" Casey shouted.

"We can't let it get away!" Raph insisted.

Raph and Casey pursued it up the stairs, but it was clear they weren't going to reach it in time. Not in a foot race to see who could get there first. The robot had gotten too much of a lead.

If they were going to destroy this bot, they'd have to work together.

Raph grabbed Casey and threw him through the

air as hard as he could. Before Casey knew what was happening, he was a human missile flying toward the Footbot. He quickly released his homemade electro-shock weapon from underneath his pads.

BZZZZZT!

Casey Jones landed on the bot and fried its malfunctioning frame. After a series of hissing pops, the exoskeleton stumbled down the stairs to the platform. Raph added a finishing touch: a *sai* right through its metallic skull.

The Footbot sputtered and finally powered down, steam and smoke billowing from its junked frame. It was offline for good, and the Turtles' location was safe.

An exhausted Casey Jones returned to Raph's side. "That . . . was . . . too close," he wheezed.

"You're a pretty good fighter," Raph admitted.

"Sure, you're raw, unfocused, dangerous, and crazy. But you're not bad."

"Thanks," Casey replied, pulling up his mask. Coming from the angriest, meanest Turtle in the world, he knew that was a huge compliment.

They slapped hands.

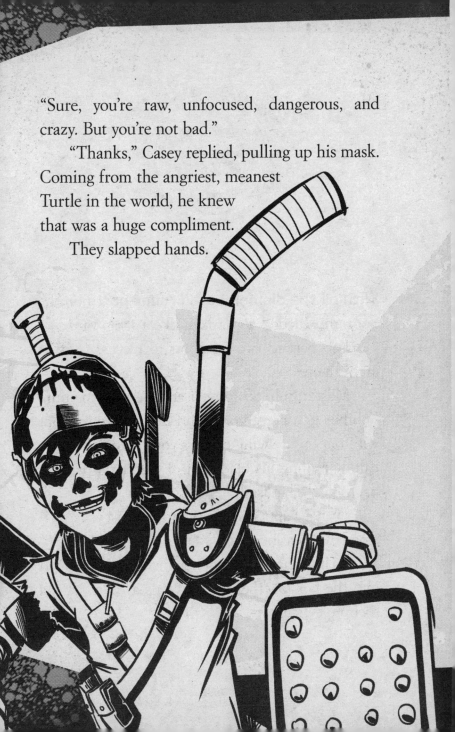

CHAPTER 28

With all the dismembered robot parts on the floor, the Turtles' lair looked like a scrap yard.

Leo hacked two Footbots to pieces. "Is that all of them?"

Master Splinter lunged at the last remaining Footbot as it crept up behind Leo. He took it out with one swift swing of his sword. "Yes," he said, calmly pulling his blade out of the bot's sparking backside. "That is all."

"What happened to Raph and Casey?" April wondered out loud.

As if on cue, April got her answer: they walked into the lair together like old pals as they relived their epic victory.

"Dude! The way we chased that thing down," Raph reminisced.

"And what about when I shocked it with my stunner!" Casey grinned. "How cool was that?"

"Don't forget the subway chase! That was the most awesome part!"

Everyone stopped cleaning up robot parts, their mouths hanging open as they gawked at the unlikely pair. What was going on here? Was this a happy Raph? Or—an even crazier thought—a *friendly* Raph?

"What's up? No more robots left for Raph and me?" Casey asked the room, leaning on his new partner-in-crime-fighting.

Mikey was perplexed. "Whoa . . . what's up with you two? You're like best friends forever now or something?"

"I see you have found a new ally, Raphael," Master Splinter observed.

"Yeah," Raph admitted. "Casey's cool."

Master Splinter came forward to express his gratitude to Casey. "Thank you for helping my family."

"No problem, rat-dude," Casey answered, still a little leery of the giant rat standing before him. "But now," he said, turning to Raph, "it's time to clean the scum off the streets."

"Let's do this!" Raph growled.

"Yeaaaahhhh!" the dangerous duo yelled simultaneously, banging their heads together.

"Great. You know what this means?" Donnie said with a tremble in his voice. "Now we have *two* Raphaels!"

Raph and Casey hit the surface as a team, ready to deal a double dose of pain to evildoers everywhere!